by Harry Allard

illustrated by Ned Delaney

HarperTrophy
A Division of HarperCollins*Publishers*

The art was drawn with pen and ink and colored with watercolor dyes and colored pencils.

THE CACTUS FLOWER BAKERY

First Harper Trophy edition, 1993.

Library of Congress Cataloging-in-Publication Data
Allard, Harry.
The Cactus Flower Bakery/ by Harry Allard ; illustrated by Ned Delaney.
p. cm.
Summary: A nearsighted armadillo meets an ostracized snake in the desert and, not realizing what kind of animal she is, helps her open a bakery.
ISBN 0-06-020046-4. — ISBN 0-06-020047-2 (lib. bdg.)
ISBN 0-06-443297-1 (pbk.)
[1. Snakes—Fiction. 2. Armadillos—Fiction. 3. Bakers and bakeries—Fiction. 4. Deserts—Fiction.] I. Delaney, Ned, ill.
II. Title.
PZ7.A413Cac 1991
[E]—dc20
90-36565
CIP
AC

A Scott Foresman Edition
ISBN 0-673-80091-1

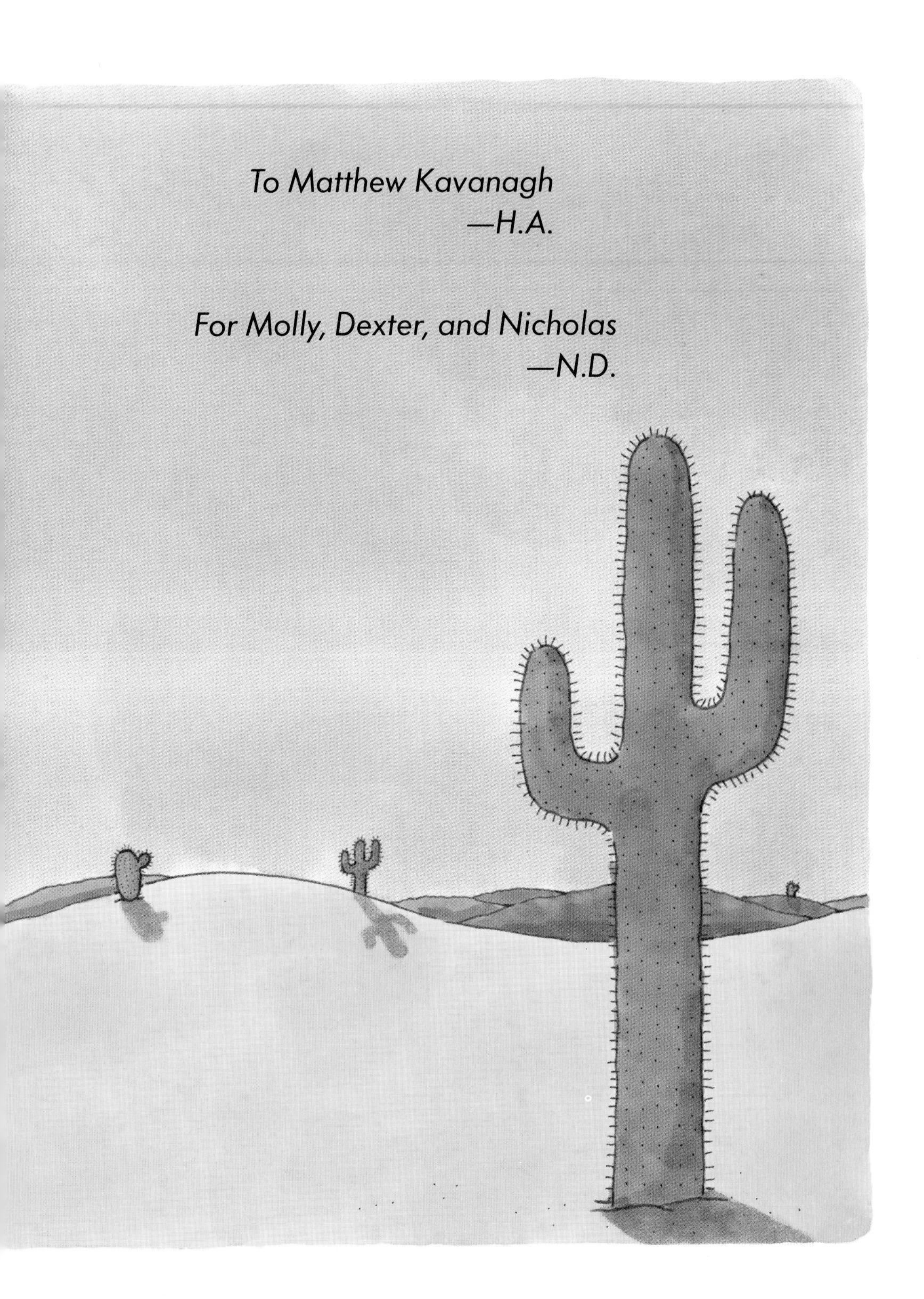

To Matthew Kavanagh
—H.A.

For Molly, Dexter, and Nicholas
—N.D.

Sunny MacFarland lived in a beautiful hole
in the middle of the Texas desert.
Life in the desert was pleasant,
but Sunny was lonely.
She didn't have any neighbors or friends.
She often wondered why.

One day an old jackrabbit came ambling by on his mule.

"Yoo-hoo!" Sunny called out. "How about a nice big glass of iced tea? And I've just baked a batch of oatmeal cookies...."

The jackrabbit took one look at Sunny, dug in his spurs, and fled in a cloud of dust.

"Odd," Sunny said to herself as she slipped back into her hole.

Sunny

A week later Sunny saw an old tortoise bicycling in her direction.

"Would you like a nice cold glass of lemonade?" Sunny asked.

"Why..., yes..., dear...," the tortoise stuttered, rummaging through her purse for her glasses.

The tortoise took a good look at Sunny.
"Aaah...!" she screamed and pedaled away just as fast as her old tortoise legs would pedal.

Sunny was terribly hurt.
Why, she wondered, did everyone run away from her?

Then one day about a month later, Sunny spotted a figure weaving across the desert.
"Hello!" she called out without much hope.
"Well, hello there!" replied the armadillo.
"Would you mind if I dropped in and rested for a while?"
"Come right in," said Sunny.

"My name," the armadillo said between bites of Sunny's cloud-light lemon chiffon pie, "is Stewart B. Preston. I'm a mailman. But ever since I broke my beautiful aviator glasses, I haven't been able to deliver the mail. I can't see where I'm going."

"You poor thing," said Sunny. "Do have another piece of pie."
"I can't quite see your face, but you've got a lovely voice," Stewart said. "Tell me, Sunny, just what kind of an animal are you anyway?"
"Would you like a Black Cow, Stewart?" Sunny asked.
"What's that?" Stewart asked.
"A generous scoop of French vanilla ice cream in a tall frosty glass of root beer," Sunny explained.

Sunny and Stewart chitchatted the day away, and before they knew it, it was night.
It was too dark for Stewart to walk back to Dallas, especially without his glasses.

"You are welcome to spend the night here," Sunny said.
"Why, that sounds like a splendid idea," said Stewart.
Humming merrily, Sunny made up the bed in her neat little guest room.

Stewart stayed another day, then a week,
then a month.
He and Sunny had so much to talk about.
They also played a lot of games together.
And between the talks and the games, they ate a lot of Sunny's cakes, cookies, pies, and macaroons.

One day as Sunny was whipping up an angel food cake, Stewart said, "Sunny, we ought to open a bakery. You could bake and I could sell."
"Why, Stewart, that's a brilliant idea!"

BUGS
Dried Flies
Angel

The Cactus Flower Bakery did a booming business.

CACTUS
FLOWER
BAKERY

By the end of the week Stewart and Sunny had made a lot of money.

Now it was Sunny's turn to have a brilliant idea.
"Stewart," she said, "I think we have enough money to buy you a new pair of aviator glasses."
Stewart was thrilled.

Dried
Flies

It took almost two weeks for Stewart's glasses to arrive from Fort Worth.

Stewart was so excited that Sunny had to help him untie the string from the box.
"Try them on," Sunny said.
Stewart did.

He looked at the sky.

Then he looked at the desert.

Then he looked at Sunny.

Stewart screamed and bolted for the door.

Sunny had never been so hurt in her whole life.
She stopped baking.
She stopped eating.

Finally Sunny took to her bed.
She just lay there with her eyes closed.
Each day Sunny grew thinner.

One day there was a timid knock at the door.
But Sunny was too weak even to whisper "come in."
There was another knock at the door, harder this time.
The door opened.
There were footsteps in the hall, then the sound of footsteps on the stairs.

"Sunny," said a familiar voice, "I'm so ashamed of myself."
Sunny opened her eyes and saw Stewart.
She was overjoyed, though she didn't have the strength to say so.

Stewart nursed Sunny back to health with ginger ale and macaroons and never did go back to Dallas.

He gave up his job as a mailman to stay in the desert with Sunny.

What's more, Stewart explained to all the desert creatures what a kind and gentle snake Sunny really was.

Sunny and Stewart still live together in the desert.
If you're ever on Route 126 heading toward El Paso,
stop in at their bakery. The lemonade is always cold,
and the cake is the best in Texas.